Stopping by Woods on a Snowy Evening

DUTTON CHILDREN'S BOOKS * NEW YORK

ROBERT FROST
Stopping by Woods on a Snowy Evening

Illustrated by Susan Jeffers

LIBRARY OF CONGRESS CATALOGING-IN-PUBLICATION DATA

Frost, Robert, 1874-1963.
Stopping by woods on a snowy evening.
Summary: Illustrations of wintry scenes accompany each line of the well-known poem.
[1. Winter—Poetry.   2. American Poetry]
1. Jeffers, Susan.   II. Title.
PZ8.3F937St   1978   811'.5'2   78-8134   ISBN: 0-525-46734-3

Published in the United States by Dutton Children's Books,
a division of Penguin Young Readers Group
345 Hudson Street, New York, New York 10014
www.penguin.com

Editor: Stephanie Lurie   Designer: Alyssa Morris
Manufactured in China

10

For Judes the jewel

$\mathscr{W}$hose woods these are I think I know.

His house is in the village, though;

He will not see me stopping here
To watch his woods fill up with snow.

My little horse must think it queer
To stop without a farmhouse near

Between the woods and frozen lake
The darkest evening of the year.

He gives his harness bells a shake
To ask if there is some mistake.

The only other sound's the sweep

Of easy wind

and downy flake.

The woods are lovely, dark and deep,

But I have promises to keep,

And miles to go before I sleep,

And miles to go before I sleep.

There is only one thing more majestic than a Robert Frost poem about snow—a snowstorm itself.

While I was growing up, snowstorms were highly anticipated events in my family. My mother's favorite thing to do was simply to walk outside and look. She was a painter, and my first painting lessons came from her. They were really lessons in looking. She would ask me: What is the color of the tree shadow? Is it blue? Blue green? Violet? And what is the shape of the highlight on the copper teakettle? Oval? Square? Diamond? She was teaching me to paint what I saw, not what I knew. What I knew could never be enough.

During the winter that I drew the pictures for *Stopping by Woods on a Snowy Evening*, nature obliged by delivering two record snowstorms in Westchester County. In addition, I was living on a small farm surrounded by snowy fields and frozen ponds. Wherever I looked, a line of the poem was illustrated.

How fortunate for me.

—Susan Jeffers